This book belongs to

....

TOVE JANSSON'S
MOOMIN BOOKS

*The main series are being reissued by Sort Of Books
in special Collectors' Editions during 2017–18.*

TWO MOOMIN STORIES
FOR OXFAM

This special edition of two Moomin
stories is published in October 2017
in support of Oxfam by

SORT OF BOOKS
PO Box 18678, London NW3 2FL
www.sortof.co.uk

Printed and bound in Italy by
L.E.G.O. S.p.A. on Forest
Certified Paper (FSC)

A CIP catalogue record for this book
is available from the British Library.
ISBN 978-1-908745-74-3

TWO MOOMIN STORIES

THE INVISIBLE
CHILD

AND

THE FIR TREE

TOVE JANSSON

CONTENTS

THE INVISIBLE
CHILD

THE INVISIBLE CHILD

ONE DARK AND RAINY EVENING the Moomin family sat around the verandah table picking over the day's mushroom harvest. The big table was covered with newspapers, and in the centre of it stood the lighted kerosene lamp. But the corners of the verandah were dark.

"Little My has been picking pepper mushrooms again," Moominpappa said. "Last year she collected flybane."

"Let's hope she takes to chanterelles next autumn," said Moominmamma. "Or at least to something not actually poisonous."

"Hope for the best and prepare for the worst," Little My observed with a chuckle. They continued their work in peaceful silence.

Suddenly there were a few light taps on the glass pane in the door, and without waiting for an answer Too-Ticky came in and shook the rain off her oilskin jacket. Then she held the door open and called out in the dark: "Well, come along!"

"Whom are you bringing?" Moomintroll asked.

"It's Ninny," Too-Ticky said. "Yes, her name's Ninny." She still held the door open, waiting. No one came.

"Oh, well," Too-Ticky said and shrugged her shoulders. "If she's too shy she'd better stay there for a while."

"She'll be drenched through," said Moominmamma.

"Perhaps that won't matter much when one's invisible," Too-Ticky said and sat down by the table. The family stopped working and waited for an explanation.

"You all know, don't you, that if people are frightened very often, they sometimes become invisible," Too-Ticky said and swallowed a small egg mushroom that looked like a little snowball. "Well. This Ninny was frightened the wrong way by a lady who had taken care of her without really liking her. I've met this lady, and she was horrid. Not the angry sort, you know, which would have been understandable. No, she was the icily ironical kind."

"What's ironical?" Moomintroll asked.

"Well, imagine that you slip on a rotten mushroom and sit down on the basket of newly picked ones," Too-Ticky said. "The natural thing for your mother would be to be angry. But no, she isn't. Instead she says, very coldly: "I understand that's your idea of a graceful dance, but I'd thank you not to do it in people's food." Something like that."

"How unpleasant," Moomintroll said.

"Yes, isn't it," replied Too-Ticky. "This was the way this lady used to talk. She was ironic all day long every day, and finally the kid started to turn pale and fade around the edges, and less and less was seen of her. Last Friday one couldn't catch sight of her at all. The lady gave her away to me and said she really couldn't take care of relatives she couldn't even see."

"And what did you do to the lady?" My asked with bulging eyes. "Did you bash her head?"

"That's of no use with the ironic sort," Too-Ticky said. "I took Ninny home with me, of course. And now I've brought her here for you to make her visible again." There was a slight pause. Only the rain was heard, rustling along over the verandah roof. Everybody stared at Too-Ticky and thought for a while.

"Does she talk?" Moominpappa asked.

"No. But the lady has hung a small silver bell around her neck so that one can hear where she is." Too-Ticky arose and opened the door again. "Ninny!" she called out in the dark.

The cool smell of autumn crept in from the garden, and a square of light threw itself on the wet grass. After a while there was a slight tinkle outside, rather hesitantly. The sound came up the steps and stopped. A bit above the floor a small silver bell was seen hanging in the air on a black ribbon. Ninny seemed to have a very thin neck.

"All right," Too-Ticky said. "Now, here's your new family. They're a bit silly at times, but rather decent, generally speaking."

"Give the kid a chair," Moominpappa said. "Does she know how to pick mushrooms?"

"I really know nothing at all about Ninny," Too-Ticky said. "I've only brought her here and told you what I know. Now I

17

have a few other things to attend to. Please look in some day, won't you, and let me know how you get along. Cheerio."

When Too-Ticky had gone the family sat quite silent, looking at the empty chair and the silver bell. After a while one of the chanterelles slowly rose from the heap on the table. Invisible paws picked it clean from needles and earth. Then it was cut to pieces, and the pieces drifted away and laid themselves in the basin. Another mushroom sailed up from the table.

"Thrilling!" My said with awe. "Try to give her something to eat. I'd like to know if you can see the food when she swallows it."

"How on earth does one make her visible again," Moominpappa said worriedly. "Should we take her to a doctor?"

"I don't think so," said Moominmamma. "I believe she wants to be invisible for a while. Too-Ticky said she's shy. Better leave the kid alone until something turns up."

And so it was decided.

The eastern attic room happened to be unoccupied, so Moominmamma made Ninny a bed there. The silver bell tinkled along after her upstairs and reminded Moominmamma of the cat that once had lived with them. At the bedside she laid

out the apple, the glass of juice and the three striped pieces of candy everybody in the house was given at bedtime.

Then she lighted a candle and said: "Now have a good sleep, Ninny. Sleep as late as you can. There'll be tea for you in the morning any time you want. And if you happen to get a funny feeling or if you want anything, just come downstairs and tinkle."

Moominmamma saw the quilt raise itself to form a very small mound. A dent appeared in the pillow. She went downstairs again to her own room and started looking through her granny's old notes about Infallible Household Remedies. Evil Eye. Melancholy. Colds. No. There didn't seem to be anything suitable. Yes, there was. Towards the end of the notebook she found a few lines written down at the time when Granny's hand was already rather shaky. "If people start getting misty and difficult to see." Good. Moominmamma read the recipe, which was rather complicated, and started at once to mix the medicine for little Ninny.

* * *

The bell came tinkling downstairs, one step at a time, with a small pause between each step. Moomintroll had waited for it all morning. But the silver bell wasn't the exciting thing. That was the paws. Ninny's paws were coming down the steps. They were very small, with anxiously bunched toes. Nothing else of Ninny was visible. It was very odd.

Moomintroll drew back behind the porcelain stove and stared bewitchedly at the paws that passed him on their way to the verandah. Now she served herself some tea. The cup was raised in the air and sank back again. She ate some bread and butter and marmalade. Then the cup and saucer drifted away to the kitchen, were washed and put away in the closet. You see, Ninny was a very orderly little child.

21

Moomintroll rushed out in the garden and shouted: "Mamma! She's got paws! You can see her paws!"

'I thought as much,' Moominmamma was thinking where she sat high in the apple tree. 'Granny knew a thing or two. Now when the medicine starts to work we'll be on the right way.'

"Splendid," said Moominpappa. "And better still when she shows her snout one day. It makes me feel sad to talk with people who are invisible. And who never answer me."

"Hush, dear," Moominmamma said warningly. Ninny's paws were standing in the grass among the fallen apples.

"Hello Ninny," shouted My. "You've slept like a hog. When are you going to show your snout? You must look a fright if you've wanted to be invisible."

"Shut up," Moomintroll whispered, "she'll be hurt." He went running up to Ninny and said: "Never mind My. She's

hard-boiled. You're really safe here among us. Don't even think about that horrid lady. She can't come here and take you away…"

In a moment Ninny's paws had faded away and become nearly indistinguishable from the grass.

"Darling, you're an ass," said Moomin-mamma. "You can't go about reminding the kid about those things. Now pick apples and don't talk rubbish."

They all picked apples.

After a while Ninny's paws became clearer again and climbed one of the trees.

It was a beautiful autumn morning. The shadows made one's snout a little chilly but the sunshine felt nearly like summer. Everything was wet from the night's rain, and all colours were strong and clear. When all the apples were picked or shaken down, Moominpappa carried the biggest apple mincer out in the garden, and they started making apple-cheese.

Moomintroll turned the handle, Moominmamma fed the mincer with apples and Moominpappa carried the filled jars to the verandah. Little My sat in a tree singing the Big Apple Song.

Suddenly there was a crash.

On the garden path appeared a large heap of apple-cheese, all prickly with glass splinters. Beside the heap one could see Ninny's paws, rapidly fading away.

"Oh," said Moominmamma. "That was the jar we use to give to the bumblebees. Now we needn't carry it down to the field. And Granny always said that if you want the earth to grow something for you, then you have to give it a present in the autumn."

Ninny's paws appeared back again, and above them a pair of spindly legs came to view. Above the legs one could see the faint outline of a brown dress hem.

"I can see her legs!" cried Moomintroll.

"Congrats," said Little My, looking down out of her tree. "Not bad. But the Groke knows why you must wear snuff-brown."

Moominmamma nodded to herself and sent a thought to her Granny and the medicine.

Ninny padded along after them all day. They became used to the tinkle and no longer thought Ninny very remarkable.

By evening they had nearly forgotten about her. But when everybody was in bed Moominmamma took out a rose-pink shawl of hers and made it into a little dress. When it was ready she carried it upstairs to the eastern attic room and cautiously laid it out on a chair. Then she made a broad hair ribbon out of the material left over. Moominmamma was enjoying herself tremendously. It was exactly like sewing dolls' clothes again. And the funny thing was that one didn't know if the doll had yellow or black hair.

* * *

The following day Ninny had her dress on. She was visible up to her neck, and when she came down to morning tea she bobbed and piped: "Thank you all ever so much."

The family felt very embarrassed, and no one found anything to say. Also it was hard to know where to look when one talked to Ninny. Of course one tried to look a bit above the bell where Ninny was supposed to have her eyes. But then very easily one found oneself staring at some of the visible things further down instead, and it gave one an impolite feeling.

Moominpappa cleared his throat. "We're happy to see," he started, "that we see more of Ninny today. The more we see, the happier we are…"

Little My gave a laugh and banged the table with her spoon. "Fine that you've started talking," she said. "Hope you have anything to say. Do you know any good games?"

"No," Ninny piped. "But I've heard about games."

Moomintroll was delighted. He decided to teach Ninny all the games he knew.

After coffee all three of them went down to the river to play. Only Ninny turned out to be quite impossible. She bobbed and nodded and very seriously replied, "Quite" and "How funny" and "Of course", but it was clear to all that she played only from politeness and not to have fun.

"Run, run, can't you!" My cried. "Or can't you even jump?"

Ninny's thin legs dutifully ran and jumped. Then she stood still again with arms dangling. The empty dress neck over the bell was looking strangely helpless.

"D'you think anybody likes that?" My cried. "Haven't you any life in you? D'you want a biff on the nose?"

"Rather not," Ninny piped humbly.

"She can't play," mumbled Moomintroll.

"She can't get angry," Little My said. "That's what's wrong with her. Listen, you," My continued and went close to Ninny with a menacing look. "You'll never have a face of your own until you've learnt to fight. Believe me."

"Yes, of course," Ninny replied, cautiously backing away.

* * *

There was no further turn for the better.

At last they stopped trying to teach Ninny to play. She didn't like funny stories either. She never laughed at the right places. She never laughed at all, in fact. This had a depressing effect on the person who told the story. And she was left alone to herself.

30

Days went by, and Ninny was still without a face.

They became accustomed to seeing her pink dress marching along behind Moominmamma. As soon as Moominmamma stopped, the silver bell also stopped, and when she continued her way the bell began tinkling again. A bit above the dress a big rose-pink bow was bobbing in thin air.

Moominmamma continued to treat Ninny with Granny's medicine, but nothing further happened. So after some time she stopped the treatment, thinking that many people had managed all right before without a head, and besides perhaps Ninny wasn't very good-looking.

Now everyone could imagine for themselves what she looked like, which can often brighten up a relationship. One day the family went off through the wood down to the beach. They were going to pull the boat up for winter. Ninny came tinkling behind as usual, but when they came in view of the sea she suddenly stopped. Then she lay down on her stomach in the sand and started to whine.

"What's come over Ninny? Is she frightened?" asked Moominpappa.

"Perhaps she hasn't seen the sea before," Moominmamma said. She stooped and exchanged a few whispering words with Ninny. Then she straightened up again and said: "No, it's the first time. Ninny thinks the sea's too big."

"Of all the silly kids," Little My started, but Moominmamma gave her a severe look and said: "Don't be a silly kid yourself. Now let's pull the boat ashore."

They went out on the landing-stage to the bathing hut where Too-Ticky lived, and knocked at the door. "Hullo," Too-Ticky said, "how's the invisible child?"

"There's only her snout left," Moominpappa replied. "At the moment she's a bit startled, but it'll pass over. Can you lend us a hand with the boat?"

"Certainly, Too-Ticky said.

While the boat was pulled ashore and turned keel upwards, Ninny had padded down to the water's edge and was standing immobile on the wet sand. They left her alone.

Moominmamma sat down on the landing-stage and looked down into the water. "Dear me, how cold it looks," she said. And then she yawned a bit and added that nothing exciting had happened for weeks.

Moominpappa gave Moomintroll a wink, pulled a horrible face and started to steal up to Moominmamma from behind.

Of course, he didn't really think of pushing her in the water as he had done many times when she was young. Perhaps he didn't even want to startle her, but just to amuse the kids a little.

But before he reached her a sharp cry was heard, a pink streak of lightning shot

over the landing-stage and Moominpappa let out a scream and dropped his hat into the water. Ninny had sunk her small invisible teeth in Moominpappa's tail, and they were sharp.

"Good work!" cried My. "I couldn't have done it better myself!"

Ninny was standing on the landing-stage. She had a small, snub-nosed, angry face below a red tangle of hair. She was hissing at Moominpappa like a cat.

"Don't you dare push her into the big horrible sea!" she cried.

"I see her, I see her!" shouted Moomin-troll. "She's sweet!"

"Sweet, my eye," said Moominpappa, inspecting his bitten tail. "She's the silliest, nastiest, badly brought-uppest child I've ever seen, with or without a head."

He knelt down on the landing-stage and tried to fish for his hat with a stick. And in some mysterious way he managed to tip himself over, and tumbled in on his head.

He came up at once, standing safely on the bottom, with his snout above water and his ears filled with mud.

"Oh dear!" Ninny was shouting. "Oh, how great! Oh, how funny!" The landing-stage shook with her laughter.

"I believe she's never laughed before," Too-Ticky said wonderingly. "You seem to have changed her; she's even worse than Little My. But the main thing is that one can see her, of course."

"It's all thanks to Granny," Moomin-mamma said.

THE FIR TREE

THE FIR TREE

ONE OF THE HEMULENS was standing on the roof, scratching at the snow. He had yellow woollen mittens that after a while became wet and disagreeable. He laid them on the chimney top, sighed and scratched away again. At last he found the hatch in the roof.

"That's it," the Hemulen said. "And down there, they're lying fast asleep. Sleeping and sleeping and sleeping. While other people work themselves silly just because Christmas is coming."

He was standing on the hatch, and as he couldn't remember whether it opened inwards or outwards he stamped on it, cautiously. It opened inwards at once, and the Hemulen went tumbling down among snow and darkness and all the things the Moomin family had stowed away in the attic for later use.

The Hemulen was now very annoyed and furthermore not quite sure of where he had left his yellow mittens. They were his favourite pair.

So he stumped down the stairs, threw the door open with a bang and shouted in a cross voice: "Christmas is coming! I'm tired of you and your sleeping, and now Christmas will be here almost any day!"

The Moomin family was hibernating in the drawing-room as they were wont to do. They had been sleeping for a few months already and were going to keep it up until spring. A sweet sleep had rocked them through what felt like a single long summer afternoon. Now all at once a cold draught disturbed Moomintroll's dreams. And someone was pulling at his quilt and shouting that he was tired and Christmas was coming.

"Is it spring already?" Moomintroll mumbled.

"Spring?" the Hemulen said nervously. "I'm talking about Christmas, don't you know, Christmas. And I've made absolutely no arrangements yet myself and here they send me off to dig you out. I believe I've lost my mittens. Everybody's running about like mad and nothing's ready…"

The Hemulen clumped upstairs again and went out through the hatch.

"Mamma, wake up," Moomintroll said anxiously. "Something awful is happening. It's called Christmas."

"What d'you mean?" his mother said and thrust her snout out from under her quilt.

"I don't really know," her son replied. "But nothing seems to be ready, and something's got lost, and everyone is running about like mad. Perhaps there's a flood again."

He cautiously shook the Snork Maiden by the shoulder and whispered: "Don't be afraid, but something terrible's happening."

"Eh," Moominpappa said. "Easy now."

He rose and wound the clock that had stopped somewhere in October.

Then they followed the Hemulen's wet trail upstairs and climbed out on to the roof of the Moominhouse.

The sky was blue as usual, so this time it couldn't be the volcano. But all the valley was filled with wet cotton, the mountains and the trees and the river and the roof. And the weather was cold, much colder than in April.

"Is this white stuff Christmas?" Moominpappa asked wonderingly. He scooped up some of the cotton in his paw and peered at it. "I wonder if it's grown out of the ground," he said. "Or fallen down from the sky. If it came all at once, that must have been most unpleasant."

"But Pappa, it's snow," Moomintroll said. "I know it is, and it doesn't fall all at the same time."

"No?" Moominpappa said. "Unpleasant all the same."

The Hemulen's Aunt passed by the house with a fir tree on her chair-sledge.

"So you're awake at last," she observed casually. "Better get yourself a fir before dark."

"But why?" Moominpappa began to say.

"I haven't time to explain now," the Hemulen's Aunt called back over her shoulder and quickly disappeared.

"Before dark, she said," the Snork Maiden whispered. "The danger comes by dark, then."

"And you need a fir tree for protection," Moominpappa mused. "I don't understand it."

"Nor I," Moominmamma said submissively. "Put some woollen socks and scarves on when you go for the fir. I'll make a good fire in the stove."

* * *

Even if disaster was coming, Moominpappa decided not to cut down one of his own firs, because he was particular about them. Instead he and Moomintroll climbed over Gaffsie's fence and chose a big fir that she wouldn't have any use for.

"Is the idea to hide oneself in it?" Moomintroll wondered.

"I don't know," Moominpappa said and swung his axe. "I don't understand a thing."

They were almost by the river on their way back when Gaffsie came running towards them with a lot of parcels and paper bags in her arms. She was red in the face and highly excited, so, thankfully, she did not recognise her fir tree.

"Stuff and bother!" Gaffsie cried. "Badly brought-up hedgehogs should never be allowed to … And as I've told Misabel, it's a shame…"

"The fir," Moominpappa said, desperately clinging to Gaffsie's fur collar. "What does one do with one's fir?"

"Fir," Gaffsie repeated confusedly. "Fir? Oh, it's such a nuisance! It's a horrid thing … I haven't dressed mine yet … How on earth can I find the time?"

She dropped several parcels in the snow, her cap slipped askew and she was near to tears from nervous exhaustion.

Moominpappa shook his head and took hold of the fir again.

* * *

At home Moominmamma had dug out the verandah with a shovel and laid out life-belts, aspirin, Moominpappa's old gun and some warm compresses. One had to be prepared.

A small Woodie was sitting on the outermost edge of the sofa, with a cup of tea in its paws. It had been sitting in the snow below the verandah, looking so miserable that Moominmamma had invited it in.

"Well, here's the fir," Moominpappa said. "If

we only knew how to use it. Gaffsie said it had to be dressed."

"We haven't anything large enough," Moominmamma said worriedly. "Whatever did she mean?"

"What a beautiful fir," the small woody cried and swallowed some tea the wrong way from pure shyness, regretting already that it had dared to speak.

"Do you know how to dress a fir tree?" the Snork Maiden asked.

The Woodie reddened violently and whispered: "In beautiful things. As beautifully as you can. So I've heard." Then, overwhelmed by its shyness, it clapped its paws to its face, upset the teacup and disappeared through the verandah door.

"Now keep quiet a moment, please, and let me think," Moominpappa said. "If the fir tree is to be dressed as beautifully as possible, then it can't be in order to hide it. The idea must be to placate the danger in some way. I'm beginning to understand."

They carried the fir out into the garden and planted it firmly in the snow. Then they started to decorate it all over with the most beautiful things they could think of.

They adorned it with the big shells from the summertime flower-beds, and with the Snork Maiden's shell necklace. They took the prisms from the drawing-room chandelier and hung them from the branches, and at the very top they pinned a red silk rose that Moominpappa had once upon a time given Moominmamma as a present.

Everyone brought the most beautiful thing they had to placate the incomprehensible

powers of winter. When the fir tree was dressed, the Hemulen's Aunt passed by again with her chair-sledge. She was steering the other way now, and her hurry was still greater.

"Look at our fir tree," Moomintroll called to her.

"Dear me," said the Hemulen's Aunt. "But then you've always been a bit unlike other people. Now I must ... I haven't the least bit of food ready for Christmas yet."

"Food for Christmas," Moomintroll repeated. "Does he eat?"

The Aunt never listened to him. "You don't get away with less than a dinner at

51

the very least," she said nervously and went whizzing down the slope.

Moominmamma worked all afternoon. A little before dark she had the food cooked for Christmas, and served in small bowls around the fir tree. There was juice and yoghurt and blueberry pie and eggnog and other things the Moomin family liked.

"Do you think Christmas is very hungry?" Moominmamma wondered, a little anxiously.

"No worse than I, very likely," Moomin-pappa said longingly. He was sitting in the snow with his quilt around his ears, feeling a cold coming on. But small creatures always have to be very, very polite to the great powers of nature.

Down in the valley everyone's windows were lighting up. Candles were lit under the trees and in every nest among the branches, and flickering candle flames went hurrying through the snowdrifts. Moomintroll gave his father a questioning look.

"Yes," Moominpappa said and nodded. "It's best we prepare for all eventualities."

So Moomintroll went into the house and collected all the candles he could find. He planted them in the snow around the fir tree and cautiously lit them, one after the other, until they formed a little circle of flames to placate the darkness and Christmas. After a while everything seemed to quieten down in the valley; probably everyone had gone home to await what was coming. One single lonely shadow was wandering among the trees. It was the Hemulen.

"Hello," Moomintroll called softly. "Is he coming?"

"Don't disturb me," the Hemulen replied sullenly, looking through a long list in which nearly every line seemed to be crossed out.

He sat down by one of the candles and started to count on his fingers. "Mother, Father, Gaffsie," he mumbled. "The cousins … the eldest hedgehog … I can leave out the small ones. And Sniff gave me nothing last year. Then Misabel and Whomper, and Auntie, of course … This drives me mad."

"What is it?" the Snork Maiden asked anxiously. "Has anything happened to them?"

"Presents," the Hemulen exclaimed. "More and more presents every time Christmas comes around!" He scribbled a shaky cross on his list and ambled off.

"Wait!" Moomintroll shouted. "Please explain … And your mittens…"

But the Hemulen disappeared in the dark, like all the others. Everyone seemed to be in a terrible hurry and worrying about the coming of Christmas.

So the Moomin family quickly went in to look for some presents. Moominpappa chose his best trolling-spoon which had a very beautiful box. He wrote 'For Christmas' on the box and laid it out in the snow. The Snork Maiden took off her ankle ring and sighed a little as she rolled it up in silk paper.

Moominmamma opened her secret drawer and took out her book of paintings, the one and only coloured book in all the valley.

Moomintroll's present was so lavish and private that he showed it to no one. Not even afterwards, in the spring, did he tell anyone what he had given away.

Then they all sat down in the snow again and waited for the frightening guest.

Time passed, and nothing happened.

Only the small Woodie who had upset the cup of tea appeared from behind the woodshed. It had brought all its relations and the friends of these relations, and each of them was just as small and grey and miserable and frozen.

"Happy Christmas," the Woodie shyly whispered.

"You're the first to suggest Christmas is happy," Moominpappa said. "Aren't you at all afraid of what's going to happen when it comes?"

"But this is it," the Woodie mumbled and sat down in the snow with its relations. "May we look? You've got such a wonderful fir tree."

"And all the food," one of the relations said dreamily.

"And real presents," said another.

"I've dreamed all my life of seeing this up close," the Woodie said with a sigh.

There was a pause. The candles burnt steadily in the quiet night. The Woodie and its relations sat quite still. One could feel their admiration and longing, stronger and stronger, and finally Moominmamma edged a little closer to Moominpappa and whispered: "Don't you think so, too?"

"Why, yes, but if..." Moominpappa objected.

"No matter," Moomintroll said. "If Christmas gets angry, we can close the doors and perhaps we'll be safe inside."

Then he turned to the Woodie and said: "You can have it all."

The Woodie didn't believe its ears at first. It stepped cautiously closer to the fir tree, with its whiskers trembling. Then all of its friends and relations followed.

They had never had a Christmas of their own before.

"I think we'd better be off now," Moominpappa said anxiously.

They padded back to the verandah, locked the door and hid under the table. Nothing happened.

After a while they looked anxiously out of the window.

All the small creatures were sitting around the fir tree, eating and drinking and opening parcels and having more fun than ever. Finally they climbed the fir tree and carefully fastened the burning candles on the branches.

"Only there ought to be a star at the top," the Woodie's uncle said.

"Do you think so?" the Woodie replied, looking thoughtfully at Moominmamma's red silk rose. "What difference does it make so long as the idea's right?"

"The rose should have been a star," Moominmamma whispered to the others. "But how on earth..?"

They looked at the sky, black and distant but unbelievably full of stars, a thousand times more than in summer. And the biggest one was hanging exactly above the top of their fir tree.

"I'm sleepy," Moominmamma said. "I'm really too tired to wonder about the meaning of all this. But it seems to have come off all right."

"At least I'm not afraid of Christmas any more," Moomintroll said. "I believe the

Hemulen and his Aunt and Gaffsie must have misunderstood the whole thing."

They laid the Hemulen's yellow mittens on the verandah rail where he'd be sure to catch sight of them, and then they went back to the drawing-room to sleep some more, waiting for the spring.

A MOOMIN GALLERY

Compiled by **PHILIP ARDAGH**

MEET THE MOOMINS, THEIR FRIENDS
and OTHER CREATURES

THE MOOMIN FAMILY

THE ANCESTOR

The Ancestor is the oldest member
of the Moomin family. We all have
ancestors but, rather unusually, the
Moomin's ancestor is still alive.
Much hairier than the modern-
day Moomins, he doesn't speak, swings from
pictures, and lives in and around their stove. He
generally shuns company, liking to stay out of sight.

MOOMINPAPPA

As a baby, Moominpappa was found in a shopping
bag on the steps of the Moomin Foundling
Home. After an adventurous youth, he becomes a
responsible husband, father and home
owner. Practical with his paws, he loves his
family and sailing but is forever
seeking something just beyond
the horizon until, finally, he comes
to realise that he can be himself in
the heart of his family.

BY PHILIP ARDAGH

MOOMINMAMMA

Moominmamma is an amazing mother, not just
to her own son, Moomintroll, but also to the ever-
increasing extended family that lives in and around
the Moominhouse. She is the Moomin who can make
things right; can calm and protect. On
the inside, of course, she has her
own fears and sometimes longs
for solitude, but is forever putting
others first. She knows the true
values in life and is rarely seen
without her handbag.

MOOMINTROLL

Young and adventurous – and despite facing floods,
high winds and even a fiery comet – Moomintroll
takes happiness for granted, such is the love in the
Moomin family. While content to be
alone, Moomintroll is a devoted
and loyal friend, and is Snufkin,
the Snork Maiden and Sniff's
closest ally. He leads a life of
lazy days and adventure.

FRIENDS & REGULARS

SNIFF

Sniff is the first creature to be adopted by the Moomins, and Moomintroll is like a big brother to him. Though not quite so brave, Sniff still likes an adventure, and, despite being a bit greedy (especially when it comes to gems!), he likes to share his discoveries. But he does want credit where credit's due. Sniff loves his toy dog, Cedric. All in all, he's like a typical young child, and he does find a lot of very useful things!

SNUFKIN

Solitary and self-contained, Snufkin has few possessions – just his beloved mouth organ and the contents of his knapsack. If he wants something, he simply carries it in his head. Moomintroll's best friend, he leaves Moomin Valley every November and travels south, returning in spring. He dislikes authority in the form of notices telling you what NOT to do, and park-keepers. He hates park-keepers!

LITTLE MY

Little My is small. Tiny, in fact. But that's on the outside. She is BIG on personality and a force to be reckoned with. Fiercely loyal to her friends, she is brave, independent and can be direct to the point of rudeness. Little My is a strong, independent young Mymble who just happens to be able to sleep comfortably in a sewing basket.

THE SNORK MAIDEN

To the Snork Maiden, looks are all-important. She is proud of her golden fringe, and often wears a flower behind her ear or a bow in her tail. She always wears her golden ankle bracelet. Like all Snorks, she changes colour as she changes her emotions (whereas Moomins always remain white). She can be practical and ingenious when she needs to be and sees herself as Moomintroll's girlfriend.

THE SNORK

The Snork could not be more different to his sister, the Snork Maiden. He likes to record everything in exercise books (preferably ones with squared, rather than lined, paper). He thinks of himself as a great organiser and wants things to be solved by committee (as long as he's in charge of it). He really is a bit of a know-all, but does genuinely seek knowledge. And he's a big fan of machinery and inventions.

THE MUSKRAT

The Muskrat moves in with the Moomins when Moominpappa accidentally destroys his riverside home. He's a philosopher; a deep thinker. His favourite book is *The Uselessness of Everything*, though he finds plenty of use for the Moomins' hammock. The victim of practical jokes from young Moomintroll and friends, Muskrat wants to be left in peace! (His most undignified moment is when he accidentally sits on a cake with lots of icing.)

THE MYMBLE'S DAUGHTER AND MYMBLES

The Mymble's daughter (the eldest of the Mymble's many children) loves being a Mymble from head to toe. She's independent and responsible because she's used to helping look after her younger siblings. Lots of them. In truth there are dozens and dozens of them, one of them being Little My. Over time, the Mymble's daughter also gets called 'the Mymble' which can be confusing, what with it being her mother's name!

TOO-TICKY

Too-Ticky is competent, self-assured and happy with her own company, though she does share her home – the Moomins' bathhouse – with invisible shrews. She doesn't hibernate in winter, and introduces this snow-covered world to Moomintroll when he wakes up early one year. Too-Ticky welcomes in spring with her barrel organ and helps others discover their own strengths and abilities

69

through trial and error, though she also knows that not everything which gets broken can be mended.

HEMULENS

Hemulens are usually figures of authority – jailers, park-keepers, police officers – or they're collectors of, say, butterflies, stamps or botany. Hemulens in authority wear their uniform with pride. Hemulen collectors wear dresses. The last thing a Hemulen wants is to complete his collection. Then he's just an owner, with nothing more to collect. Then there's the other kind of much rarer Hemulen, who's hale and hearty and LOUD and likes to play sport ... and teach others the rules.

FILLYJONKS

The Moomins encounter many a Fillyjonk and the one thing most have in common, apart from looking anxious, is that they feel anxious. Look at a shelf of ornaments and a Fillyjonk worries about dusting them or accidentally breaking them. Hear the wind rustling in the breeze and they may fear that their whole house will be blown away. Cleaning and tidying plays a BIG part in most Fillyjonks' lives.

MOOMINPAPPA'S OLD FRIENDS

THE MUDDLER

The scatter-brained Muddler lives in a Maxwell House coffee tin which he shares with his collection of junk and discarded bits and bobs. These include old buttons, which he's forever losing. He marries the Fuzzy and is Sniff's father.

HODGKINS

Hodgkins, the Muddler's uncle, is Moominpappa's oldest friend. Something of an inventor, he builds the *Ocean Orchestra*, a river boat renamed the *Oshun Oxtra* when the Muddler paints it spelled that way on the side. It is in this boat that Moominpappa has some of his first real adventures.

THE JOXTER

Both relaxed and
worry-free,
the phrase 'laid
back' could have

been invented for the Joxter. You can tell at a glance
that he and Snufkin are related. They are father and
son. The Joxter has the same disregard for authority
and rules as Snufkin, too.

SOME LESS FAMILIAR FACES

THE WHOMPER

Whompers are quiet,
unassuming, sincere creatures.
The Whomper who lives on
a floating theatre with the
Moomin family is a nervy fellow
and, when frightened by an
unexplained THUMP, blindly
strikes out with a wooden
sword. Despite his fearing the
worst, no one is hurt.

WOODIES

Woodies are small, many and childlike.
At one stage, a group of Woodies
seems to adopt Snufkin as their
father when he takes a
stand against the
Hemulen park-
keeper who's
always out to
spoil their fun.

TOFT

Toft is a Whomper, and
don't let anyone tell you
different. A mysterious
chap, he lives under an
upturned boat and idolises
Moominmamma. His
most unusual trait,
however, is that some
of the wonderfully
imaginative stories he
tells himself seem to come true...

MISABEL

Even Misabel's name sounds miserable, which is exactly what she is. Misabel is always worried that others won't think she's good enough at whatever it is she's doing, and is very sad inside. But, despite all this – or, perhaps, because of it – she proves to be a very good actor.

THINGUMY AND BOB

These two little creatures turn up in Moomin Valley with a large suitcase, which contains the King's

Ruby. They speak in a coded language, mixing the first letters of words ("Man you cake it out?" "Mot nutch').

SOMEWHAT FEARED FOLK

THE HOBGOBLIN

Although the Hobgoblin may seem frightening with his big eyes and flowing cape, and his riding through the skies on the back of a great panther, and although he is a mighty magician on a quest to find an enormous ruby, he is, in fact, a rather friendly old gentleman who does enjoy a good pancake.

HATTIFATTENERS

The Hattifatteners grow from seeds. In thunderstorms, they give off sting-like electric

shocks. Deaf and speechless, they travel in large groups, seemingly without emotion. They are listless, forever travelling, forever seeking something. Whenever they visit an island, they leave a scroll at its highest point. Once a year, they congregate on Lonely Island, where they gather around a barometer hanging from a pole. No one knows why.

THE GROKE

Feared by most, the Groke is possibly the only one of her kind. She craves warmth and light and possibly even company, but wherever she sits, nothing ever grows. She may extinguish a bonfire, not to spoil

the fun or to create darkness but in her endless quest to get the chill out of her bones. Few, if any, feel sorry for this melancholy creature with her frightening grimace and deep, lonely eyes.

EDWARD THE BOOBLE

Edward – who is a Booble – is possibly
and probably the biggest animal in and
around Moomin Valley. He has the most
unfortunate habit of stepping
on other creatures and killing
them, which usually makes

him cry for a week. He does insist on paying for their
funerals, though. Edward is very happy when he wins
first prize for 'porcelain destruction' (china-smashing)
at the Hemulen's theme park, whether he did it on
purpose or not.

THE ANT-LION

Ant-lions can be found in many parts of the world.
None has such an impressive leonine head as the
Ant-lion who digs holes in the beach in Moomin
Valley, though. And flicks sand. More
of an annoyance than a threat.
Moomintroll and the Snork
trick the Ant-lion into the
Hobgoblin's hat ... where he
re-emerges as a hedgehog.

NIBLINGS

The hairy little nose-chewing Niblings have the rare distinction of carrying off the Hemulen's Aunt, a relative of the Hemulen who runs the Foundling Home that Moominpappa escapes from. Moominpappa is briefly concerned for her welfare but it transpires that the Niblings love the Aunt because she holds multiplication contests. And it turns out that the Niblings LOVE maths! Everyone ends up happy.

This Moomin Gallery – featuring just some of the marvellous characters in Tove Jansson's books – was especially compiled for this Oxfam edition by Philip Ardagh, author of THE WORLD OF MOOMIN VALLEY: A DEFINITIVE GUIDE TO THE MOOMINS, published by Macmillan Children's Books.

SHARE THE GIFT OF THE MOOMINS

Anyone who reads Tove Jansson's timeless story *The Invisible Child* will experience how her isolated heroine takes her rightful place in the world when she becomes a part of the Moomin family.

In 2017, when you're still more likely to be poor if you're a woman, Jansson's themes of tolerance, inclusiveness and respect are more important than ever. This is the inspiration behind a campaign partnering Oxfam, Moomin Characters, Sort Of Books and Waterstones.

This special edition of *The Invisible Child* is published in support of Oxfam projects empowering women and girls worldwide with job opportunities, a stronger voice in society and freedom from violence.

OXFAM